To my grandson, Chama,
in hopes that his generation will
swim in an ocean full of life.

No More Plastic in the Ocean!

Written by
Lavinia Currier

Illustrated by
Mollie Ginther

Scripta

Honolulu, Hawai'i

but it's no fun here for my friends and me anymore.

Plenty plastic, 'ōpala every day!

People dump it in the water, and flush it out the pipes,

it chokes us, tangles, breaks and mangles

and never goes away!

I change colors when I feel

scared,

worried,

I see the moon Mahina rise
in my pretty blue glass float
that once was used on a fishing boat.

"Mahina, will you kōkua, oh most wise?"

Mahina sighs, "Oh! What a pity! All this plastic from the city.

I'll blow it back there while they sleep—

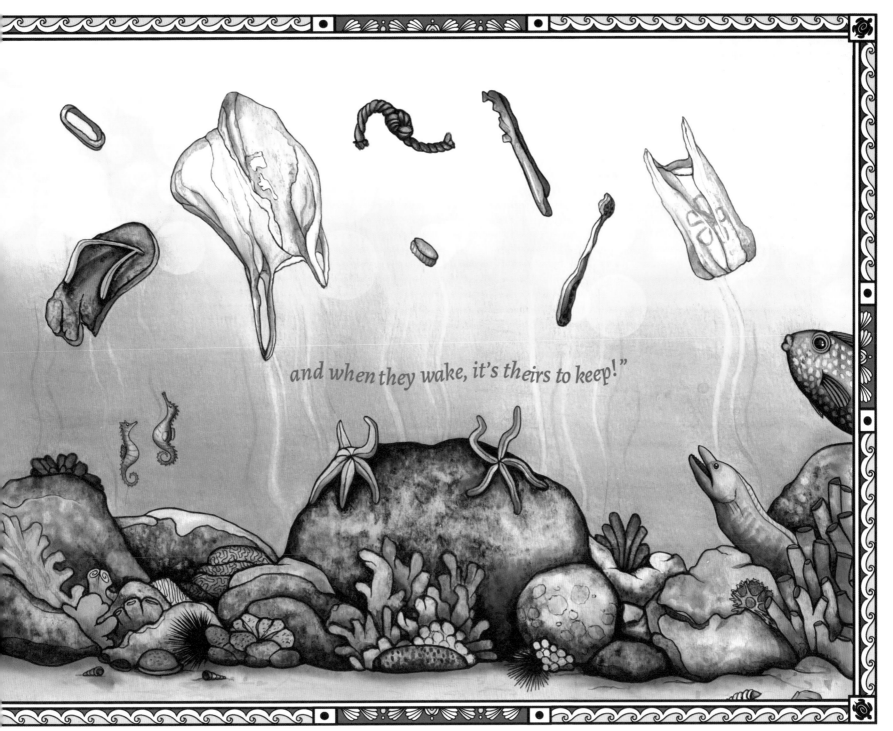

and when they wake, it's theirs to keep!"

Mahina strings up plastic trash on lei
and calls out to 'iwa birds across the bay.

Out of the waves, and high,
high in the sky they fly.

The 'iwa drop their trashy cargo down on buildings, trees, and all around.

Everything *is* covered, head to toe.

Nothing is working, no one can go.

The 'opihi picker stumbles,

the plane's propeller tangles,

everybody grumbles,

tripping, snarling, falling,
raining plastic everywhere!

Gangs of flip-flops chasing dogs,

the mongoose make a dash—

empty bottles stick on those

who threw them in the trash!

Smelly piles *lie* in the sun
spoiling all the children's fun.

It turns out humans also
don't like plastic by the ton!

Do you think that people had no notion their trash would end up in the ocean?

Little Lani greets me, shaking hands with my eight legs,

"Can't you make the plastic go away, He'e?" she begs.

I call Mahina once again, go whisper in her ear,

"Do you think they've learned   from all this fuss,

that if *there* is *no ocean, there is no 'us'?"*

Mahina nods,

"I'll turn the plastic into flowers,

'ulu and banana,

if the people promise to mālama.

Please— no more throwing your ʻōpala

in our one and only Moana!"

Lani waves "Mahalo, He'e, and Mahina too—

now it's time for bed, I'll dream of you"

I'm sad to say 'a hui hou' to my new friend, but my ocean friends swim near.

"Come back into the water, He'e", they call, "we can see the coast is clear."

Glossary of Hawaiian Words

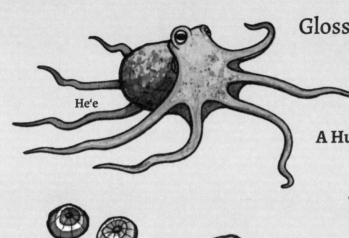

He'e

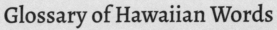

Lei

'Iwa

A Hui Hou - until we meet again

He'e - octopus

'Iwa - Great Frigatebird

Kōkua - help

Kuleana - responsibility

Laulima - cooperate/work together

Lei - garland

'Ōpala - garbage

Mahalo - thank you

Mahina - moon

Mālama - take care

Moana - ocean

'Opihi - limpet

'Ulu - breadfruit

'Opihi

'Ulu

Mahina

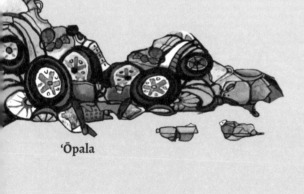

'Ōpala

Moana

About the Author

About the Illustrator

Lavinia Currier is a poet, film writer/director, conservationist and eco-activist.

She lives between the mainland and Hawai'i, where she is involved in land stewardship and protection of the coastal areas on the east end of Molokai. Many mornings she and her grandson pick up plastic on the beach, joining Sustainable Coastlines, Nature Conservancy, and other concerned citizens in an effort to protect marine life from the dangers of our industrial plastic waste.

Mollie Ginther is an author and illustrator with a focus on children's and young adult literature. She has a passion for visual storytelling and is always looking for creative twists on daily life to bring unusual and new stories to the table.

Mollie received her Bachelor of Fine Arts degree in drawing and painting from the University of Wisconsin-Madison. Despite growing up in the Midwest, Mollie has always had a deep love for the ocean and all its inhabitants. She has since spent a lot of time living in and around Hawai'i and the Pacific Ocean, forming an even deeper connection with the sea and forever gaining inspiration for new stories.